A Faithful Tale

Bark and Serve Series

Dyslexic Friendly Edition

Written & Illustrated by

Chris E. Steele

Paper back ISBN-13: 978-1-963272-06-2

ShelteringTree.Earth, LLC Publishing
PO Box 973, Eagle Lake, FL 33839

Did you enjoy this book?
We love to hear from our readers.
Please visit the author and illustrator at
ShelteringTreeMedia.com

What is a "Dyslexic Friendly" Book?

Sheltering Tree Media has taken steps to make our books more friendly for those who live with dyslexia. While the following principles will not make every book readable for every reader, it is our best effort to create products that encourage reading and to support all readers.

Throughout the book, we use a font named OpenDyslexic. This is a free font that is designed to help dyslexic readers distinguish each letter from the others. For more information about OpenDyslexic, how it differs from other fonts, and research behind the font, visit their website: www.opendyslexic.com.

In our books created for children, we use a font size which provides the reader with plenty of spacing between the letters (which is called *kerning*). The bigger, wider font tends to be easier to the reader's eyes.

The space between each word is increased (this is called *word spacing*). This helps better to distinguish when one word ends and the next begins. The line spacing is greater than most common fonts (this is called *leading*). This all should help with readability.

Whenever possible, the text is Left-Aligned but it is not justified on the right side. Allowing the right side of a paragraph to remain *rough* keeps the word spacing consistent throughout.

Our Dyslexic Friendly books are printed on cream or ivory paper which is also thicker than the average book page. This minimizes the sharp contrast of black-on-white pages as well as bleedthrough of text from the previous page.

Finally, Sheltering Tree Media has made colored overlays available when you purchase a book through our online store. You can find these overlays at ShelteringTreeMedia.com/shop/dyslexic-friendly.

These are some of the principles we use to create a book as readable as possible to those living with dyslexia. Some may find this helpful; some may not. Please provide us with any insights you might have to improve our Dyslexic Friendly principles. We pray this will enable many to heighten their love for reading.

DEDICATION

For Dave, who humbly walks by faith.

עֵזֶר

(Helper)

[18] The Lord God also said: 'It is not good for the man to be alone. Let us make a helper for him similar to himself. [19] Therefore, the Lord God, having formed from the soil all the animals of the earth and all the flying creatures of the air, brought them to Adam, in order to see what he would call them. For whatever Adam would call any living creature, that would be its name.

Genesis 2:18-19[1]

---

[1] The Holy Bible Catholic Public Domain Version

Bitterroot Farm is owned by Mr. and Mrs. Davis.

On their farm, there's a boy named Colton, and a bunch of animals — cows, pigs, chickens, ducks, goats, sheep, horses, donkeys, and a cat.

Oh, and me! I'm their special dog.

My name is Desi, and I want to share how I came to live here on Bitterroot Farm.

Mr. and Mrs. Davis call me *Hambone*. I'm not sure why they call me that name.

I dislike ham, but I do like bones.

Let me think about why Mr. and Mrs. Davis call me *Hambone*.

Nope! I don't get why they call me that name.

Colton doesn't call me *Hambone*. As soon as I got to Bitterroot Farm, he gave me a name. He looked at me and said, "Hi, Darling Desi."

People who love you
give you loving
names.
Do your parents,
grandparents, or
friends have special
names for you?

Life was grand when I was a puppy before I came to Bitterroot Farm. My five brothers and sisters and I played with our big dogs every day.

We had so much fun chasing butterflies, swimming, and playing tag.

My mom and dad told me we were a family that helped others. I did not know what that meant.

Now and then, our home received visitors. My family always greeted visitors by rushing to the fence, sitting down, and wagging tails in welcome.

One day, a man came to visit. He stepped out of his car and greeted us with a smile. I searched for my brother Max outside, but he wasn't there.

The man entered our home. After a while, the man led Max to the car.

I was yapping "Max, Max, Max!" The big dogs all stood in a row and told him, "Be a helper and never forget that we love you."

The car went down the driveway with Max inside, and I watched. Max peeked out the back window. Max looked terrified and upset.

The very next day, while the other dogs were playing outside, I played inside the house. I heard a truck approaching the driveway.

Mr. and Mrs. Davis came to visit me inside the house.

Lifting me gently, the man with the enormous hat looked at my paws and said, "This little pup will grow up to be a big dog."

"Hi little pup, would you like to be a part of our family?" he asked me.

I felt confused because I already had a family.

Mrs. Davis wrapped me up in my cozy blanket and carried me to the truck.

At the fence stood my mom, dad, brothers, and sisters. "Be a helper and remember how much we love you," my parents told me.

I wanted to stay with my family. I was so mad, sad, and scared that I just started whining. With a hug, Mrs. Davis comforted me and said, "Everything will be alright."

What helps you
feel better when
you're angry, sad,
or scared?

It was tough to say goodbye to my family. I didn't know for sure if I'd ever see my home and family again. As the days passed, their words, "Be a helper to others" stayed with me.

The first few days, Colton showed me the farm and took great care of me. Mr. and Mrs. Davis were very busy taking care of the farm. Spending time with my boy Colton was how I filled most of my days.

Colton practiced reading books to me on the porch swing while I listened quietly. When he got stuck on a word, I waited patiently for him to sound it out.

Colton felt scared to leap from the dock. I urged him to jump into the duck pond with me using my "woofs."

To feed the animals on the farm, Mr. Davis cut our grassy fields into bales of hay and stacked them in a row. Colton climbed to the top of the first hay bale. Colton seemed like he wanted to jump to the next bale.

I jumped up and butted my head against Colton's leg. He was not moving. So, I showed him how to spring up and off onto the next bale! He looked at me and then looked down between the bales. If he didn't make it across, he was probably thinking about the big fall and getting hurt.

Yikes! He might have been thinking he didn't want to fail. I did not know why he wouldn't jump but, he just didn't jump.

But I knew he could do it, so I jumped a second time. I stood still on the bale, watching and waiting. Then, Colton closed his eyes and finally -- he jumped!

When he opened his eyes, he was standing on top of the next bale, and he had the biggest smile on his face. He jumped once more to reach me, and we shared a smile.

I loved playing with Colton every day, but by the end of the day, I was tired. My favorite part of every evening was when Mr. Davis read a book to Colton. I liked to curl up in my blanket close to the warm fire. Mr. Davis and Colton liked to snuggle together in the chair.

The stories he read were super exciting and different each night, but sometimes I struggled to stay awake to the ending.

Every night, after Mr. Davis finished a book, it was time for bed. I helped Colton say his prayers.

Angel of God, my guardian dear,
to whom God's love commits me here,
ever this night be at my side
to light and guard,
to rule and guide.

God bless our family and our farm.

Thank you for the gift
of my best friend, Darling Desi.

Amen

After Colton fell asleep, Mr. and Mrs. Davis would tiptoe to his bedroom to check on him.

One night, I heard Mrs. Davis say, "Just look at that Darling Desi. He's been an incredible helper, watching over Colton this summer while we took care of the farm."

"He's a special dog," said Mr. Davis.

And then, something stirred in me.

I remembered my parents saying, "Be a helper to others."

I thought, 'Am I the helper my parents hoped I would be?'

My heart felt warm. Yes, I am a helper!

Yippee!

As I drifted off to sleep, Mr. and Mrs. Davis said a blessing over Colton:

The LORD bless you and keep you;
The LORD make His face to shine upon you, and be gracious to you;
The LORD turn His face toward you and give you peace.
Amen

Hold on for one minute. Who is attacking my tail? Oh, it's Dirt Bag the Cat!

Next time, I'll tell you about him. I am much too tired. You need to sleep now, too. Don't forget to say your prayers.

Night night.

ABOUT THE AUTHOR & ILLUSTRATOR

Chris E. Steele's books feel like story time with Grandma for a reason: she has 10 grandkids! With a little joy and a lot of faith, Chris's books help Christian families talk to their children about how to tackle the scary things in life with a large heart guided by God's words.

Chris is on a mission to teach life lessons, all with a healthy dose of love and humor. When she's not writing, she's busy illustrating stories. If she's not doing that, she's likely shooing chipmunks away from her precious vegetable garden.

At present, she and her husband Dave live on Wisconsin's eastern coast, where they spend time walking on the boardwalks with their four-legged friend.

DISCUSSION GUIDE FOR SMALL GROUPS, CLASSES, AND INDIVIDUAL REFLECTION

DIRECTIONS: Write your answers on the lines. In the Desi shapes on the facing page, draw a picture explaining your answer.

Loss

Loss means when you don't have something anymore. It can be something you had before, like a toy, or something you wanted, like winning a game. It makes you feel sad because it's gone.[2]

1. Desi left his family and home. Have you ever lost someone or had to move to some place new? How did you feel?

_____

_____

_____

_____

---

[2] The definitions are provided by Bing Copilot and are written on a third grade readability level.

2. Why do you think Desi was so upset watching Max being taken away in the car?

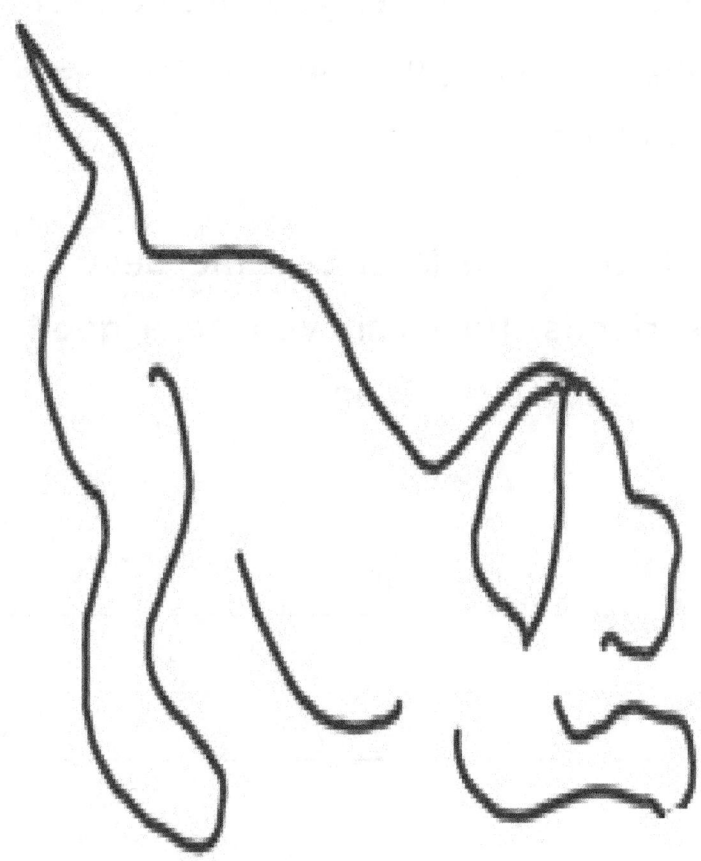

Belonging

Belonging means feeling like you are part of a group or place. It is when you feel accepted and happy to be with others. For example, you might feel belonging with your family, friends, or at school.

3. Colton and Desi became best friends. How can you be a good friend to someone?

_____

_____

_____

_____

4. What can you do to help someone new feel welcomed?

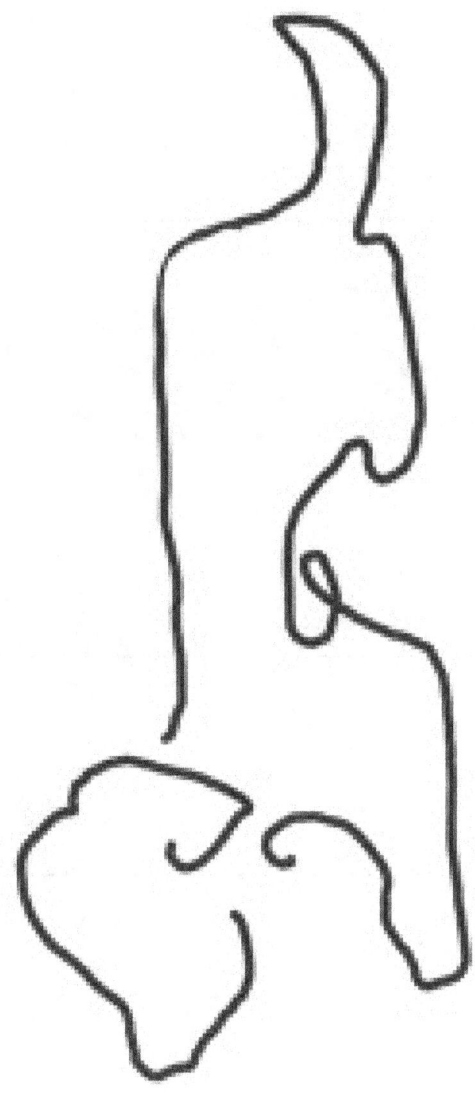

5. How does it feel when you are alone because no one asked you to play?

Learning Something New

To learn means to get new knowledge or skills. For example, when you learn to ride a bike, you are getting better at riding it. Learning can happen by reading, listening, or practicing something new.

6. Colton learned to do many new things. What do you think he was feeling when he was learning to read, jump off the dock, and leap far between bales of hay?

_____

_____

_____

_____

7. How do you feel when you are trying to learn something new? Does it help having someone show you? Who is the special person who helps you?

8. If you keep trying to do something, and cannot do it, how does that make you feel?

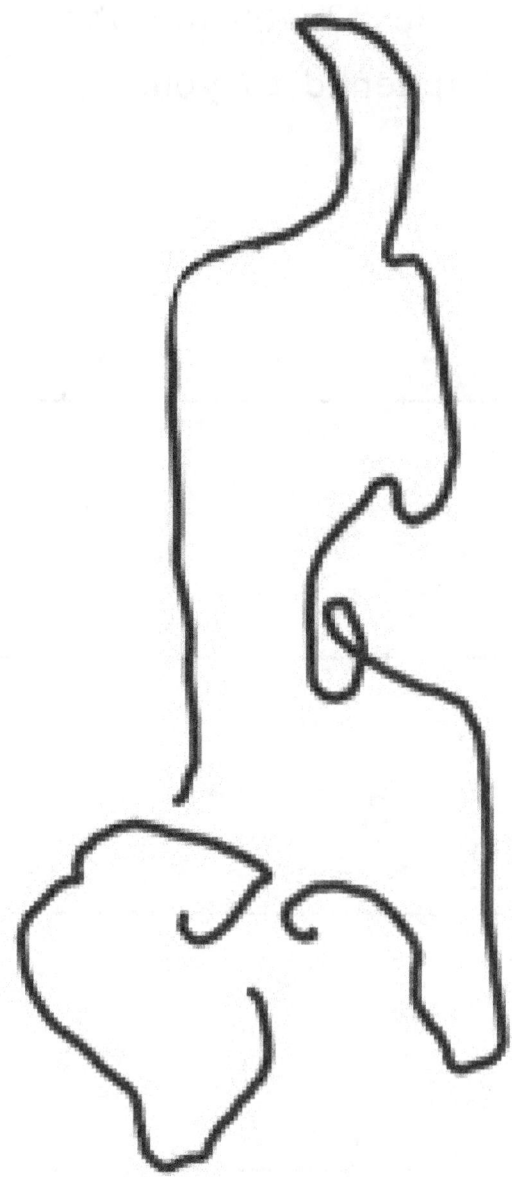

9. How do you feel when you can finally do it? Tell me about when this happened to you.

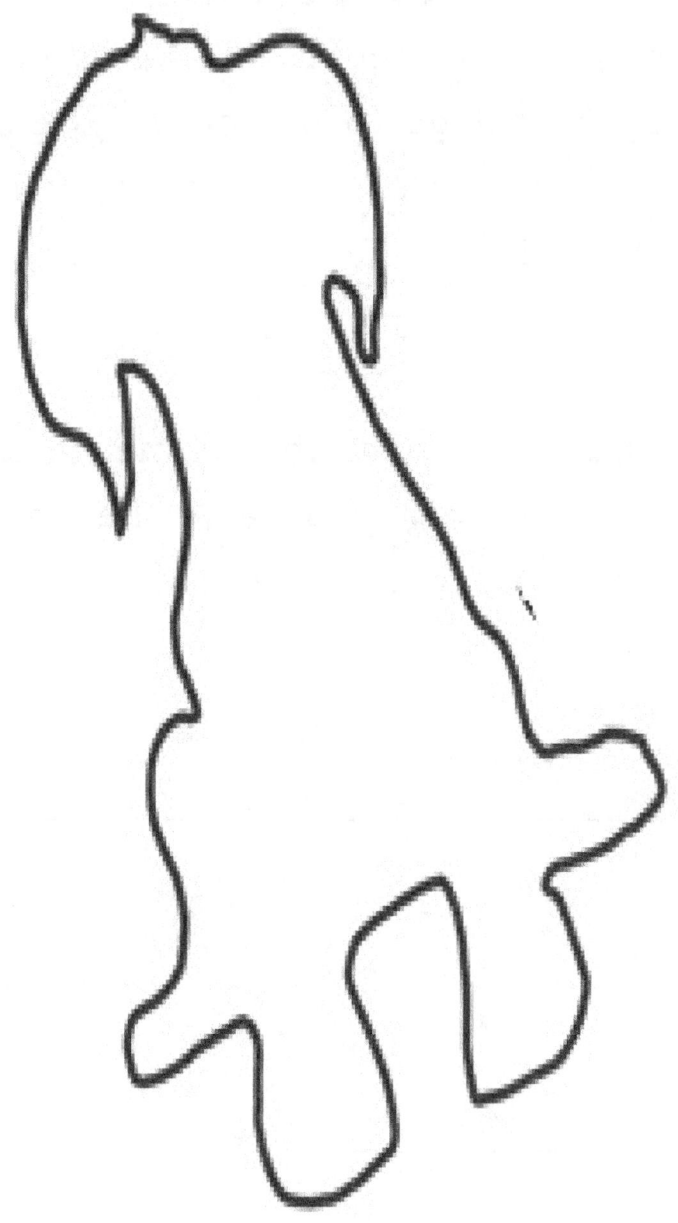

Being a Helper

A helper is someone who helps others. They do things to make things easier for other people. For example, a helper might help you clean up your toys or carry something heavy.

10. Desi learned what it meant to be a helper. Can you name the ways Desi helped on the farm?

_____

_____

_____

_____

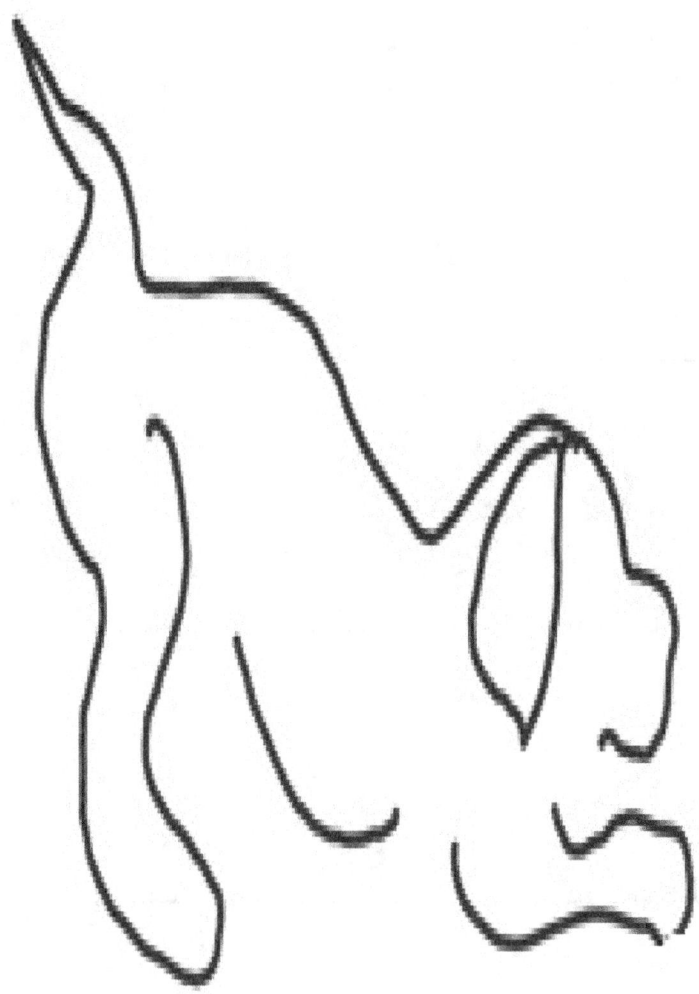

11. How does helping others make you feel?

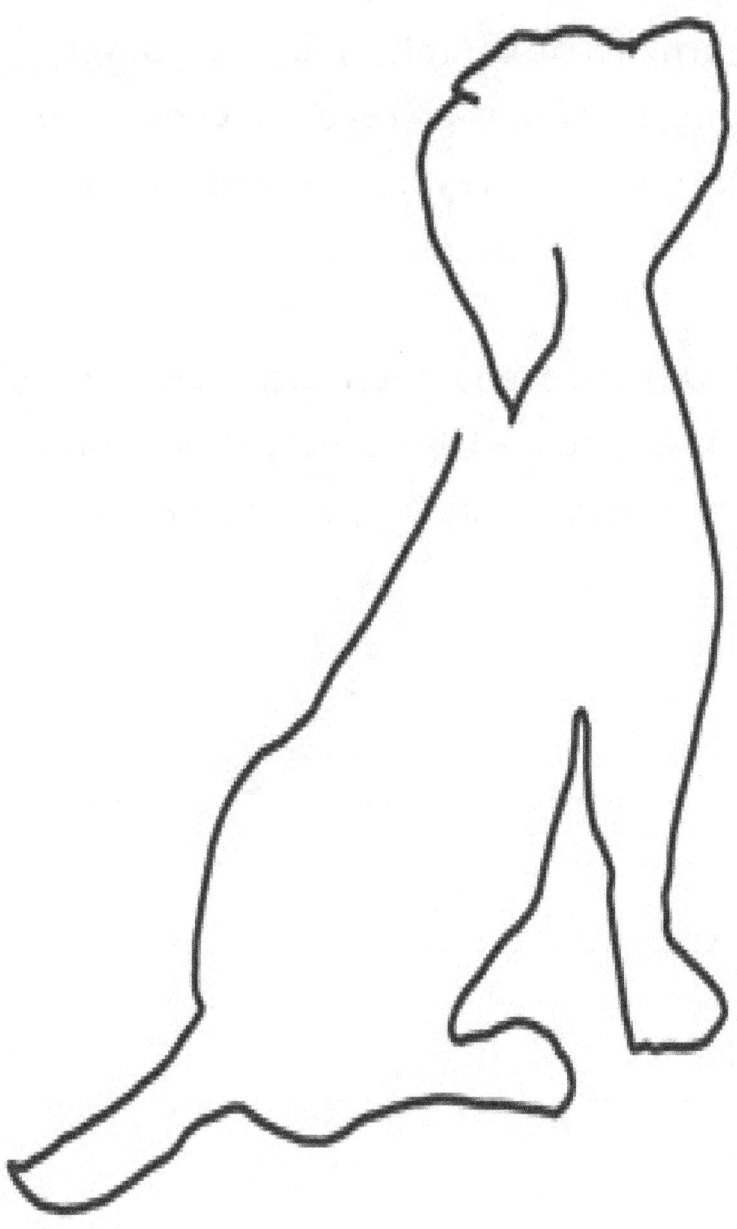

Activities

Activities are things you do for fun or to learn. For example, playing games, drawing pictures, or reading books are all activities. They are things you can do alone or with friends.

12. Describe and then draw pictures of how you can be a helper at home, in school, and at your place of worship.

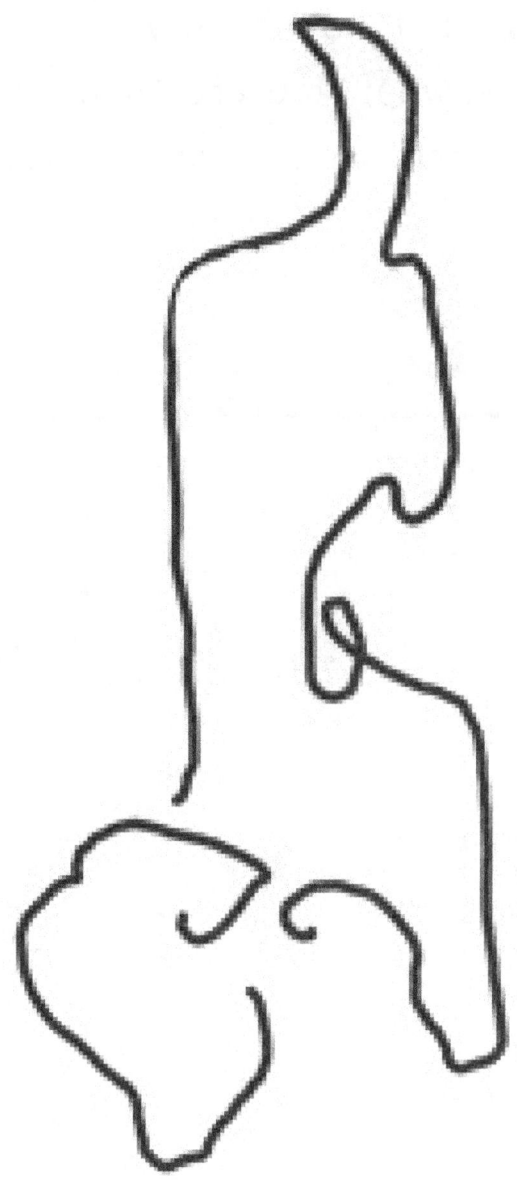

13. At bedtime, Colton, in prayer, told God what he was thankful for. Write what you are thankful for. Read this during your night prayer.

Blessing

A blessing is something good that makes you happy. It can be a kind word, a gift, or something nice that happens to you. For example, having a loving family is a blessing.

14. Find your Bible. See if you can find Numbers 6:24-26 in the Old Testament. Jesus grew up hearing and reading this very Scripture. God gave this special blessing to say over each other. Do you want to bless others with these words that have been here for three thousand years? You can! Learn this blessing and speak it to your family right before bed. Hold your hands out over the person when you speak the blessing. Copy the blessing here to help you remember it.

15. Draw and write about a time you felt proud after learning something new.

For more information,
to become one of our
authors, translators, or
illustrators,
or to contact the author and
illustrator:
ShelteringTreeMedia.com